362.2   Picard, E.
           Rafaela.
           Danger

PERMA-BOUND®   BAR: 100155

362.2   Picard, E.
           Rafaela.
           Danger

$17.90 BAR: 100155

DATE DUE	BORROWER'S NAME	RM. NO.

$17.90

PENNYCOOK
ELEMENTARY SCHOOL
3620 FERNWOOD DR.
VALLEJO, CA 94591

AR POINTS: 0.5
AR READ LVL: 4.3

The Drug Awareness Library™

Danger:
DRUGS IN YOUR
NEIGHBORHOOD

E. Rafaela Picard

The Rosen Publishing Group's
PowerKids Press™
New York

Published in 1997 by The Rosen Publishing Group, Inc.
29 East 21st Street, New York, NY 10010

First Edition

Book Design: Erin McKenna

Photo Illustrations: Cover by Seth Dinnerman; p. 20 by Sarah Friedman; all other photo illustrations by Seth Dinnerman.

Picard, E. Rafaela.
    Danger. Drugs in your neighborhood / E. Rafaela Picard.
       p. cm. — (The drug awareness library)
    Includes index.
    Summary: Explains how illegal drugs hurt people and the areas in which they live, how to detect the signs of drug use and sales in a neighborhood, and how to avoid drug dealers.
    ISBN 0-8239-5051-4
    1. Youth—Drug use—United States—Juvenile literature. 2. Drug abuse—United States—Prevention—Juvenile literature. 3. Narcotics and crime—United States—Juvenile literature. [1. Narcotics and crime.] I. Title. II. Series.
    HV5824.Y68P53 1997
    362.29'0973—dc21
                                     96-37654
                                          CIP
                                          AC

Manufactured in the United States of America

Contents

What Is a Neighborhood?

A **neighborhood** (NAY-ber-hood) is the place where someone lives. A neighborhood can be in a city, a town, or a **suburb** (SUB-urb). Your neighborhood is made up of the people who live near you. They are called neighbors. A neighborhood also includes your home, and the buildings and streets near where you live.

A neighborhood can be safe or unsafe, clean or dirty. It can also be a place where you learn a lot about life.

◀ Your neighborhood is more than just the area where you live. It's where you learn about life.

Neighborhood Lessons

Some of the things you may learn in your neighborhood are not good. You may learn that bullies get what they want. You may find out that not everyone who steals gets caught. You may also see some people use or sell drugs **illegally** (il-LEE-gul-lee). Some people think that doing these bad things is okay. But that does not make them right. These things are wrong and they do not help your neighborhood. These things do not make it safe or better. They make a neighborhood dangerous.

You may learn about some scary things, such as drugs or bullies, in your neighborhood. ▶

What Are Drugs?

Drugs are things a person can take to change the way she thinks, feels, or acts. Some drugs can help you get better when you are sick. These drugs are called medicines. Your parent or your doctor may give you medicine.

Other drugs are not medicines. They can hurt you. But people use them anyway. Many of these drugs are sold on the street. These drugs, such as marijuana, heroin, cocaine, and crack, are illegal. They are all dangerous.

◀ Your mom may give you medicine when you feel sick.

Drug Dealers

Drug dealers (DRUG DEEL-erz) are people who sell drugs. You may have seen drug dealers on the streets in your neighborhood. Drug dealers can make a lot of money by selling drugs. Sometimes they give drugs to people for free. They hope that these people will become **addicted** (uh-DIK-ted) to the drug. Someone who is addicted to a drug craves, or needs, the drug to feel normal. Drug dealers may seem nice. But they care more about making money than they do about you or the neighborhood.

Drug dealers in your neighborhood ▶
may try to get you to buy drugs.

Hurting the Neighborhood

A neighborhood where people sell or use drugs can be dangerous. Many drug dealers carry guns or knives. They may fight over the areas where they sell drugs. People who use drugs may leave sharp **syringes** (sir-RIN-jez) or broken drug **vials** (VY-ulz) made of glass in places where kids play. Drug users who are "**high**" (HY) or who need more of a drug may act strange or **violent** (VY-uh-lent). Living in a neighborhood like this can be scary.

◀ Drug dealers can make your neighborhood a scary place.

How Do Drugs Hurt You?

Drugs can make a person feel high. But drugs can also make that person feel scared, sad, or sick. Drugs can make a person see, hear, and feel things that are not real. That is how drugs change the way people act. Drugs can make people act silly, angry, scared, or violent. You never know how a drug is going to make someone act. Some drugs, such as crack, can make a person become addicted very quickly. And for some people, using a drug even once can kill them.

Using a drug can make you feel sick. ▶

Crime in Your Neighborhood

Drug users may think that they are being cool by using drugs. But they are hurting their bodies and minds and the people around them. If a drug user becomes addicted, drugs become the center of his life. The need for drugs is so strong, he may do bad things that he wouldn't normally do. He may **ignore** (ig-NOR) his family and friends. He may steal money or hurt people in his neighborhood to get more drugs.

◀ Someone who is addicted to drugs may steal money to buy more drugs.

Drugs Don't Solve Problems

People often use drugs because they want to feel better. They may believe that drugs will help them feel happy or unafraid. Getting high may be the only way they know how to forget their worries for a little while.

Everyone feels afraid or worried sometimes. That is normal. But using drugs does not solve problems. It just makes them worse. If you feel scared or worried, talk to a parent or teacher. He or she can help you solve your problems and feel better.

Using drugs won't make you feel better, but talking to an adult you trust will. ▶

Neighborhood Safety

Your neighborhood is where many of your family members and friends live. You can show that you care about your family and friends by helping to make your neighborhood safe.

One thing you can do is not to use drugs. If you use drugs now, be smart. Find an adult, such as a parent, teacher, minister, or rabbi, who can help you quit. If you don't use drugs, don't start. If you see someone selling drugs in your neighborhood, tell an adult about it.

◀ You and your parent can help make sure that your neighborhood is a safe place to be.

Taking Care of Yourself

No matter what neighborhood you live in, it is important for you to take good care of yourself. Helping yourself will also help your neighborhood.

If someone offers you drugs, stop and listen to yourself. It is up to *you* to choose what is best for you. Someone who really cares about you won't push you to do something that will hurt you. She will **respect** (ree-SPEKT) your choice not to use drugs. Tell her, "No, I don't do drugs."

22

Glossary

addicted (uh-DIK-ted) Not able to control your use of a drug.

drug dealer (DRUG DEEL-er) Someone who sells drugs illegally.

high (HY) False feeling of happiness and of having no worries when using a drug.

ignore (ig-NOR) To not pay attention to.

illegally (il-LEE-gul-ee) To do something that is against the law.

neighborhood (NAY-ber-hood) Area where someone lives.

respect (ree-SPEKT) To think highly of someone.

suburb (SUB-urb) The area just outside a city or large town.

syringe (sir-RINJ) Tube used (with a needle) to inject a drug into a person's body.

vial (VY-ul) Small bottle.

violent (VY-uh-lent) Hurting yourself or others.

23

Index